I dedicate this book to encourage
everyone to ask the tough questions.

www.mascotbooks.com

YOU ARE YOU

For more information, please contact:
Mascot Books
620 Herndon Parkway, Suite 320
Herndon, VA 20170
info@mascotbooks.com

Library of Congress Control Number: 2020920325

CPSIA Code: PRT1120A

ISBN-13: 978-1-64543-231-9

Printed in the United States

YOU ARE YOU

CASSIDY JORDAN BURKE

Illustrated by David Gnass

Pennelope goes to school with a lot of different personalities.

On Tuesdays Pennelope's class gets an extra 20 minutes of recess.

Even though Pennelope has friends, she sometimes hangs out by herself.

"Do you want to go down the slide
with me, Pennelope?"

Pennelope and Phoenix could not stop laughing and screaming with joy and excitement as they went down the slide.

Pennelope's laugh was unique. It drew a crowd.

Her "friends" started making fun of her laugh.

The whistle blew and recess was over.

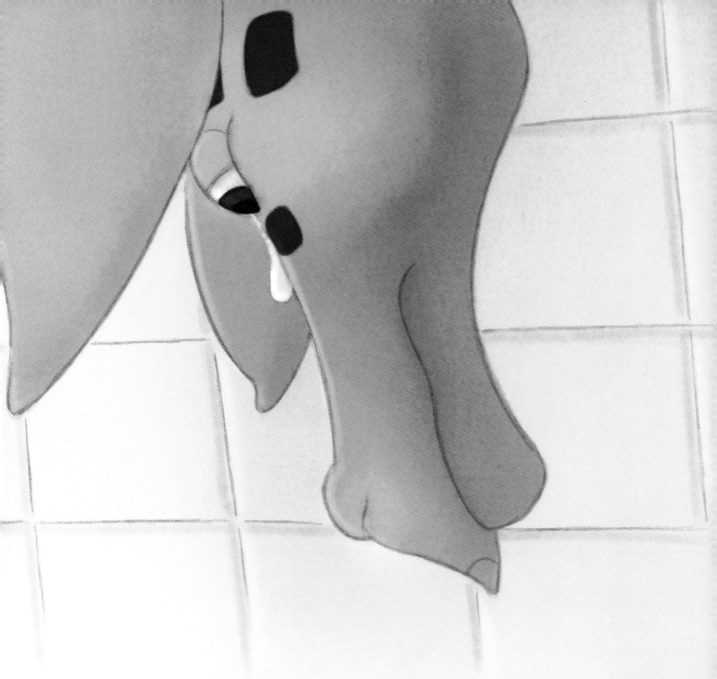

But Pennelope didn't go back to class. She was hurt by the mean words the bullies had said. She even started believing those words were true. She wondered if she'd ever be good enough to be accepted, or if she'd ever be able to get those words out of her head.

Pennelope went home after school
and went directly to bed.

For the next couple of days, Pennelope stayed in bed and didn't want to move. She didn't want to be around anyone or eat any food. She just kept replaying the hurtful actions of her classmates in her head.

Her mother assumed she was sick
and brought her soup.

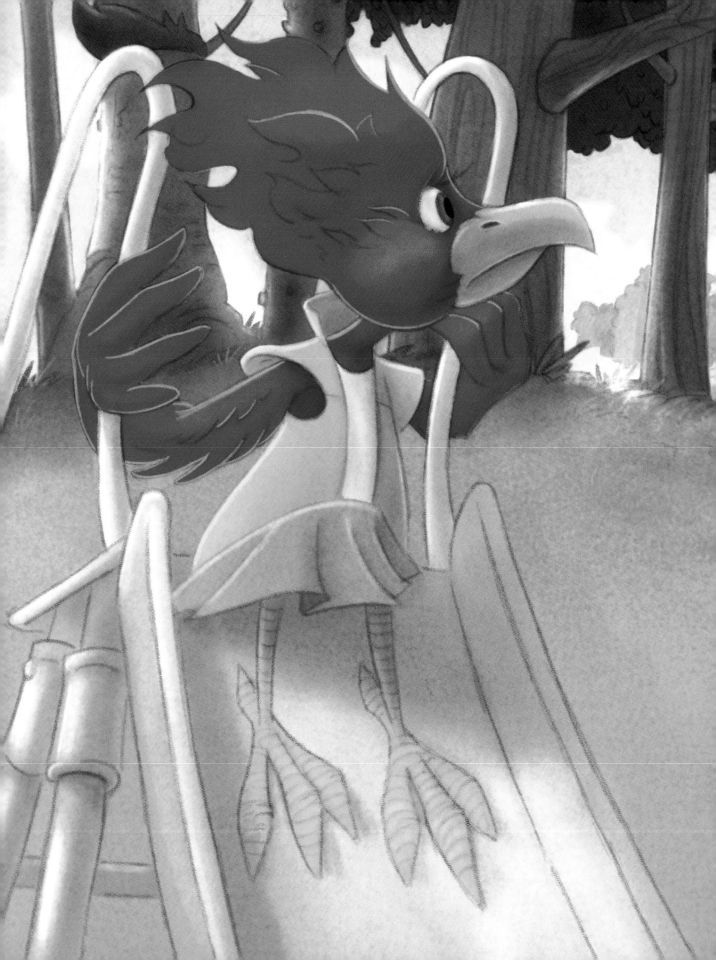

At school, Phoenix was looking forward to going down the slide with Pennelope . . . but Pennelope was not there.

What Phoenix did next was truly incredible.

Dear Friend,
You are strong. You are beautiful. You are unique. You are you! Don't let our mean classmates take away your laughter, and if you are sad, I love your laugh. I'll be waiting by I am here for you. Just want to come the tree even if you and not talk.
You are you, and you are not alone!
Phoenix
P.S.
1-800-273-8255

In that moment, Pennelope realized that this temporary problem did not deserve the power she was giving it.

She understood that she had a true friend and, most important of all, she believed that she mattered.

Although her classmates did not change their attitudes,
Pennelope decided to not let them bother her.

Pennelope thanked Phoenix for the nice note and told her
she decided that no one would take her laughter away again.

YOU ARE YOU

AND YOU ARE NOT ALONE.

CHALLENGE LETTERS

Dear parents,

Ask tough questions. Just because it's uncomfortable doesn't mean you should not talk about it. Suicide is a real issue that exists. Talk about it!

Dear friends,

There is not a formula for those who commit suicide. Don't make assumptions about your friends, especially if they are displaying any warning signs. Pay attention!

Dear teachers,

Please teach our students that it is okay not to be okay.

Dear world,

Be kind. Seek goodness and be your best—every day.

If you or someone you know is in need of help, please contact the National Suicide Prevention Lifeline, available 24/7.

1-800-273-8255

Cassidy is a leader, a coach, a mentor, a friend, and a children's book author. She strives to encourage others to live their most authentic lives and meets them exactly where they are. She was inspired to write *You Are You* to help one person. If everyone's goal was to help one person, we would live in a much different world.

Cassidy is a well-decorated academic with two bachelor's degrees and two master's degrees, but she contributes most of her learning to conversations with people and environments she has visited. As an avid traveler, she has had conversations and established friendships with people around the world who have impacted her perception and attitude about life.

Cassidy now lives in Littleton, Colorado, and works in both NCAA college athletics and the financial world. She is a light to everyone around her and hopes this book will be a tool and opportunity to make a tough conversation a little bit easier. Thank you for continuing the conversation.